IC LIBRARY
D0362196
SEP 2 8 2009

Put Beginning Readers on the Right Track with
ALL ABOARD READING™

The All Aboard Reading series is especially designed for beginning readers. Written by noted authors and illustrated in full color, these are books that children really want to read—books to excite their imagination, expand their interests, make them laugh, and support their feelings. With fiction and nonfiction stories that are high interest and curriculum-related, All Aboard Reading books offer something for every young reader. And with four different reading levels, the All Aboard Reading series lets you choose which books are most appropriate for your children and their growing abilities.

Picture Readers
Picture Readers have super-simple texts, with many nouns appearing as rebus pictures. At the end of each book are 24 flash cards—on one side is a rebus picture; on the other side is the written-out word.

Station Stop 1
Station Stop 1 books are best for children who have just begun to read. Simple words and big type make these early reading experiences more comfortable. Picture clues help children to figure out the words on the page. Lots of repetition throughout the text helps children to predict the next word or phrase—an essential step in developing word recognition.

Station Stop 2
Station Stop 2 books are written specifically for children who are reading with help. Short sentences make it easier for early readers to understand what they are reading. Simple plots and simple dialogue help children with reading comprehension.

Station Stop 3
Station Stop 3 books are perfect for children who are reading alone. With longer text and harder words, these books appeal to children who have mastered basic reading skills. More complex stories captivate children who are ready for more challenging books.

In addition to All Aboard Reading books, look for All Aboard Math Readers™ (fiction stories that teach math concepts children are learning in school); All Aboard Science Readers™ (nonfiction books that explore the most fascinating science topics in age-appropriate language); All Aboard Poetry Readers™ (funny, rhyming poems for readers of all levels); and All Aboard Mystery Readers™ (puzzling tales where children piece together evidence with the characters).

All Aboard for happy reading!

Lexile:

LSU ☑yes
SJB □yes
BL: 1.5
Pts: .5

GROSSET & DUNLAP
Published by the Penguin Group
Penguin Group (USA) Inc., 375 Hudson Street, New York, New York 10014, USA
Penguin Group (Canada), 90 Eglinton Avenue East, Suite 700, Toronto, Ontario M4P 2Y3, Canada
(a division of Pearson Penguin Canada Inc.)
Penguin Books Ltd., 80 Strand, London WC2R 0RL, England
Penguin Group Ireland, 25 St. Stephen's Green, Dublin 2, Ireland
(a division of Penguin Books Ltd.)
Penguin Group (Australia), 250 Camberwell Road, Camberwell, Victoria 3124, Australia
(a division of Pearson Australia Group Pty. Ltd.)
Penguin Books India Pvt. Ltd., 11 Community Centre, Panchsheel Park, New Delhi—110 017, India
Penguin Group (NZ), 67 Apollo Drive, Rosedale, North Shore 0632, New Zealand
(a division of Pearson New Zealand Ltd.)
Penguin Books (South Africa) (Pty.) Ltd., 24 Sturdee Avenue, Rosebank, Johannesburg 2196, South Africa

Penguin Books Ltd., Registered Offices:
80 Strand, London WC2R 0RL, England

The scanning, uploading, and distribution of this book via the Internet or via any other means without the permission of the publisher is illegal and punishable by law. Please purchase only authorized electronic editions and do not participate in or encourage electronic piracy of copyrighted materials. Your support of the author's rights is appreciated.

Based upon the animated series *Max & Ruby*
A Nelvana Limited production © 2002–2003.

Max & Ruby™ and © Rosemary Wells. Licensed by Nelvana Limited NELVANA™ Nelvana Limited. CORUS™ Corus Entertainment Inc. All Rights Reserved. Used under license by Penguin Young Readers Group.
Published in 2009 by Grosset & Dunlap, a division of Penguin Young Readers Group, 345 Hudson Street, New York, New York 10014. GROSSET & DUNLAP is a trademark of Penguin Group (USA) Inc. Manufactured in China.

Library of Congress Control Number: 2009009295

ISBN 978-0-448-45235-7 10 9 8 7 6 5 4 3 2 1

ALL ABOARD READING™

Station Stop 1

Max & Ruby™

Ruby Scores a Goal

Ruby, Roger, and Louise
are in the yard.

They are playing soccer.

Roger is the best goalie.

Max is Ruby's little brother.

He is in the yard, too.

He is playing with his robots.

The robots say,

"Alert! Alert!"

"Warning! Warning!"

"Danger! Danger!"

Louise kicks first.

Ruby cheers, "Give me an

L-O-U-I-S-E!

What does that spell?

LOUISE!"

Oh no!

Louise misses the goal.

Now it is Ruby's turn.

She will try to make a goal.

Then one robot shouts,

"Alert! Alert!"

The robot is very loud!

Ruby's kick goes wild.

Ruby is mad at Max.

"Max, your robot

made me miss the goal!

Roger is a great goalie.
I cannot score a goal
with all that noise."

Roger says,

"Try again, Ruby!"

Louise cheers for Ruby.

"Give me an R-U-B-Y!

What does that spell?

RUBY!"

"Ready! Set! Kick!"

says Ruby.

Oh no!

Look what is coming!

Ruby trips over the robot.

Her kick goes wild again.

Louise and Roger ask,

"Are you hurt?"

Ruby says,

"I am okay.

I will try one more time.

But first . . . "

Ruby goes over to Max.
"We cannot play
with your robots in the way.
Go play over there!"

Max puts his robots
in his wagon.

Then he pulls

the wagon away.

Oh no!

Two robots fall out

of the wagon.

They walk over to Ruby.

This time, Ruby hears
the robots.
She moves left.
She moves right.

The robots do not trip her.

Whap!

Ruby kicks the ball.

Oh no!

Look at what is coming!

One robot says,

"Danger! Danger!"

Roger looks around.

"What? Who is that?"

He does not watch the goal.

Whoosh!

Louise cheers for Ruby.

"Ruby scored a goal!"

Roger cheers for Ruby.

"You did it!"

Ruby is happy.

She says, "I did it!

But I had help."

Ruby gives a big cheer.

"Give me an R-O-B-O-T!

What does that spell?"

"Robot!" says Max.